Elmo's Super-Duper Birthday

By Naomi Kleinberg
Illustrated by Joe Mathieu

A Random House PICTUREBACK® Book
Random House 🏠 New York

randomhousekids.com
SesameStreetBooks.com
www.sesamestreet.org
Educators and librarians, for a variety of teaching tools, visit us at RHTeachersLibrarians.com
ISBN 978-0-399-55216-8 (trade) — ISBN 978-0-399-55217-5 (ebook)
MANUFACTURED IN CHINA
10 9 8

Elmo's birthday had almost arrived. Elmo was SO excited! It was sure to be a super-duper celebration. Elmo was having a party, and all his friends were coming.

There was a lot to do to get ready. First—the birthday cake.
"Here you go, my little chef," Mommy said. Elmo broke the eggs
carefully into the bowl and poured in the milk. Mommy stirred.

"Okay, Elmo," Mommy said. "Time to add the flour."
Elmo didn't answer. He was thinking.
"What's on your mind?" Mommy asked.
"Elmo would like to make cupcakes instead,"
he said. "Then Elmo's friends will each have
a little cake of their own."

FLOUR

"What a thoughtful idea," Mommy answered.
So Elmo and his mommy made cupcakes.
Sprinkle, sprinkle. Elmo added the sprinkles.

"What should Elmo do next?" he wondered.
Elmo helped his mommy fill the piñata with tangerines and toys, and put apples, toys, and bottles of bubbles into the goody bags. They hung up the Pin-the-Ear-on-the-Monster game. Elmo couldn't wait for tomorrow!

In the morning, Elmo and Mommy set the table—
one plate and one cup for each guest.
"Is it time yet?" Elmo asked.
"Not yet," Mommy replied.
"Is it time yet?" Elmo asked again a minute later.
Mommy sighed.
Finally the doorbell rang.

"Happy birthday, Elmo!" everyone said.

"This looks so magical!" Abby exclaimed when she saw the balloons and streamers. She gave Elmo a pink package covered with glitter.

Telly's present was shaped like a triangle. Oscar's smelled like sardines.

"I hope I have a really yucky time today," Oscar said.

First everybody played Dorothy Says.
"Glub, glub. Dorothy says, 'Hands on hips!'" said
Elmo's mommy. "Dorothy says, 'Touch your toes!'

"Dorothy says, 'Wave hello!'
Lift your foot! Hey—Dorothy
didn't say 'Lift your foot!'"

After that, everyone took a turn pulling a ribbon on the piñata. Telly's ribbon finally broke it open.

HAPPY BIRTHDAY

TM / © 2016 Sesame

TM / © 2016 Sesame

TM / © 2016 Sesame

TM / © 2016 Sesame

TM / © 2016 Sesame

TM / © 2016 Sesame

TM / 2016 © Sesame

TM / © 2016 Sesame

TM / © 2016 Sesame

TM / © 2016 Sesame

TM / 2016 © Sesame

TM / © 2016 Sesame

TM / © 2016 Sesame

TM / 2016 © Sesame

TM / 2016 © Sesame

TM / 2016 © Sesame

TM / 2016 © Sesame

TM / 2016 © Sesame

"It is raining cute little tangerines!"
Grover exclaimed. "Is that not awesome?"

The last game was Pin-the-Ear-on-the-Monster.
Funny-looking ears went all over the place.

"That's one really silly
monster!" said Big Bird,
laughing.

"Shh!" whispered Ernie. "With all those ears,
I'm sure he can hear every word we say!"

While they munched lunch, the friends talked about their own birthday parties. "After my party, we ate leftover pizza for a whole week!" Abby said.

"Cowabunga!" said Cookie Monster. "Why you not invite *me* over?"

"At my party, I popped every balloon before the guests arrived!" Oscar chimed in.

"Once I got six pairs of mittens for my birthday!" Zoe said, giggling. "I took the extras to school, for kids who didn't have any."

"I borrowed a pair of those one time," Grover remembered. "They were pink and adorable!"

When lunch was over, it was time for cupcakes. Everybody sang, "Happy birthday, dear Elmo! Happy birthday to you!"

It was time for Elmo to blow out his candles.
"Make a wish, Elmo!" Bert reminded his friend.
Elmo closed his eyes. He blew out the candles
with one big puff.

After dessert, Elmo opened his presents. Abby had given him a pot she decorated, with soil and seeds to grow herbs on the windowsill—a tiny winter garden.

Telly's gift was a game, and there was a warm red scarf from Oscar.

"It doesn't have any holes," Oscar said. "Too bad. But it looks just like your style, Fur Face!"

And there were FOUR copies of the same storybook about a little kitten. (One was from Elmo's mommy.)
"Oops!" said Bert, Ernie, and Big Bird.
"It's okay," Elmo said. "Elmo *really* likes books!"

As everyone helped clean up, Elmo whispered to his mommy. She smiled.

"Elmo wants to tell you his birthday wish, so you can help him make it come true," she said to the guests.

A little later, Elmo, his parents, and his guests arrived at the Sesame Street Community Senior Center. They brought pizza, cupcakes, piñata treats, and three brand-new copies of a storybook.

"Elmo wanted to share Elmo's birthday," the little red monster said.

"Happy birthday, Elmo," everyone called.

"Want to join us for our dance class?" asked one lady.

"Super-duper!" Elmo answered.

MAKE THE BIRTHDAY CROWN

Ask a grown-up to remove the crown from the book and help you put it together. Tape the end of one band to the left side of the crown and the end of the other band to the right, and tape the bands together in the back.

SET UP THE BIRTHDAY GAME

Remove the Pin-the-Nose-on-Elmo poster along the perforated line, and unfold it carefully.
Tape it to a wall with a lot of clear floor space around it. Remove the four Elmo noses along the perforated lines. If you need more noses to play the game, put orange construction paper under the holes left by the nose-shaped game pieces, and use a pencil to trace the shapes. Ask a grown-up to cut them out.

PLAY PIN-THE-NOSE-ON-ELMO

Give each player a game piece with some tape attached. The players will cover their eyes and, after you gently turn them around and position them in front of the poster, take turns trying to place Elmo's nose in the right spot. Have fun!